W9-BRT-864

THE AMERICAN GIRLS

1764 KAYA, an adventurous Nez Perce girl whose deep love for horses and respect for nature nourish her spirit

1774 FELICITY, a spunky, spritely colonial girl, full of energy and independence

1824 JOSEFINA, a Hispanic girl whose heart and hopes are as big as the New Mexico sky

1854 KIRSTEN, a pioneer girl of strength and spirit who settles on the frontier

1864 ADDY, a courageous girl determined to be free in the midst of the Civil War

1904 SAMANTHA, a bright Victorian beauty, an orphan raised by her wealthy grandmother

1934 KIT, a clever, resourceful girl facing the Great Depression with spirit and determination

1944 MOLLY, who schemes and dreams on the home front during World War Two

1854

Kirsten's SURPRISE

A Christmas Story

BY JANET SHAW

ILLUSTRATIONS RENÉE GRAEF

VIGNETTES PAUL LACKNER

★ American Girl™

Published by Pleasant Company Publications
Copyright © 1986, 2000 by American Girl, LLC
All rights reserved. No part of this book may be used or reproduced
in any manner whatsoever without written permission except in the
case of brief quotations embodied in critical articles and reviews.
For information, address: Book Editor, Pleasant Company Publications,
8400 Fairway Place, P.O. Box 620998, Middleton, WI 53562.

Visit our Web site at **americangirl.com**.

Printed in China.
05 06 07 08 09 LEO 49 48 47 46 45 44

American Girl™ and its associated logos, Kirsten®, and Kirsten Larson® are
registered trademarks of American Girl, LLC.

PICTURE CREDITS
The following individuals and organizations have generously given permission
to reprint illustrations contained in "Looking Back": pp. 58–59—*New Year's Eve
at Visby, 1855,* by L. O. Kinberg, Nordiska Museet, Stockholm, Sweden; *Lucia at Koberg, 1848,*
by Fritz von Dardel, Nordiska Museet, Stockholm, Sweden; p. 61—*Christmas Sheaves for the Birds,*
by Erik Johansson, Nordiska Museet, Stockholm, Sweden; p. 62—Erlander Home Museum,
Swedish Historical Society of Rockford, IL (psalmodiken, hymnal).

Cover background by Jean-Paul Tibbles

Library of Congress Cataloging-in-Publication Data

Shaw, Janet Beeler, 1937–
Kirsten's surprise: a Christmas story
(The American girls collection)
Summary: Kirsten and her family celebrate their first Christmas in their new home
on Uncle Olav's farm in mid-nineteenth-century Minnesota.
[1. Christmas—Fiction. 2. Swedish Americans—Fiction.
3. Frontier and pioneer life—Fiction]
I. Graef, Renée, ill. II. Title. III. Series.
PZ7.S53423Kj 1986 [Fic] 86-60623
ISBN 0-937295-85-X
ISBN 0-937295-19-1 (pbk.)

FOR MY MOTHER,
NADINA FOWLER

TABLE OF CONTENTS

KIRSTEN'S FAMILY
AND FRIENDS

KIRSTEN'S FAMILY

PAPA
*Kirsten's father, who
is sometimes gruff
but always loving*

KIRSTEN
*A nine-year-old
girl who moves with
her family to a new home
on America's frontier
in 1854*

MAMA
*Kirsten's mother, who
never loses heart*

LARS
*Kirsten's fourteen-year-
old brother, who is
almost a man*

PETER
*Kirsten's mischievous
brother, who is
five years old*

UNCLE OLAV
*Kirsten's uncle, who
came to America six
years before Kirsten
and her family*

LISBETH
*Kirsten's eleven-
year-old cousin*

AUNT INGER
*Kirsten's aunt, who
helps the Larsons feel
at home in America*

ANNA
*Kirsten's seven-
year-old cousin*

MISS WINSTON
*Kirsten's teacher,
who helps her
learn English*

PESTERING

 The first year that Kirsten and her family lived in the little log cabin on Uncle Olav's farm in Minnesota, the autumn weather lasted into December. Although the stream froze and they had to melt ice for water, there was only a little snow. Papa often stroked his beard and pointed to the geese flying south. "A very hard winter's on the way," he said. "It will be much colder here than in Sweden. We have to get ready for the deep snows." But Kirsten thought the traces of snow on the pines looked like the sugar Mama sprinkled on gingersnaps—light and sweet. It was hard to believe winter was coming.

One day when Kirsten came into the cabin after

school, she smelled cinnamon. "Something smells delicious," she said. "What are you making, Mama?"

Mama had her sleeves rolled up and her apron on. "It's time to bake Christmas bread," she answered. "Come help me."

Kirsten washed her hands and tied one of Mama's long aprons over her school dress. "Don't forget to cover your hands with flour so the dough won't stick," Mama said. She took several loaves of risen bread dough from the cupboard and set them on the pine table in front of Kirsten.

Kirsten pushed her fingers into the dough and punched it down. When the air was out of the dough, she shaped it into round loaves to rise a second time. The smells of yeast and spices made her mouth water.

"Will Christmas in America be just like it was in Sweden?" Kirsten asked Mama.

Mama wiped her hands on her apron. "I don't know, Kirsten. Some things here are different. And you know we don't have money for extra treats. But we'll do the best we can." Mama must have seen that Kirsten was disappointed, for she added,

2

*"Will Christmas in America be just
like it was in Sweden?" Kirsten asked.*

"Here, take a piece of dough and make a loaf of bread for your doll."

As Kirsten rolled the piece of dough between her palms, she glanced at Little Sari. Little Sari lay on Kirsten's trundle bed. She wasn't a real doll at all. She was only a worn stocking stuffed with milkweed floss. Kirsten had made her because she missed her real Sari so much. Real Sari, with her pretty face and her blue dress, was still far away in Riverton. Kirsten had to leave her there last summer, when all the money Papa had saved for their trip to America was gone. He couldn't hire a wagon to carry their trunks, so they'd left most of their things in a warehouse and walked the last twenty miles to Uncle Olav's farm.

"I wish I had my real Sari," Kirsten said. She set the little doll loaf of bread on the wooden tray with the big loaves Mama had shaped.

"I know you miss your doll," Mama said. "But work comes before play. We needed both your hands to carry tools and blankets that day." Mama's voice softened. "And you'll see Sari again soon. Mr. Berkhoff sent word that the trunks have been shipped as far as his store in Maryville. When Papa

has time, he can take the wagon
and get them."

"Oh, could he go today?"
Kirsten asked happily.

"Maryville is ten miles away, Kirsten," Mama
said. "It will take Papa half a day to get there and
back with the wagon. It's too late to go today."

"Will he go tomorrow?"

"No, Kirsten," Mama said. "He won't have time
tomorrow."

"Couldn't we just ask him?" Kirsten said.

"It would only make him cross to ask," Mama
said. "Papa is too busy now."

"When *will* Papa have time?" Kirsten knew she
was pestering Mama, but she wanted the trunks and
Sari so badly that she couldn't help herself.

Mama leaned across the table to brush flour
off Kirsten's nose. "You know Papa and Uncle Olav
have to get the farm ready for winter. That comes
first. Be patient a little while longer, Kirsten."

"Well, why don't you and I take the wagon and
get the trunks? You know how to drive the horse
and wagon, Mama!"

Now Mama smiled. "You're full of ideas today!

But there's school for you tomorrow, and we aren't strong enough to lift those big trunks. We can get along with what we have until Papa has his work done."

"But don't you want the shawl Mormor made for you, and your candlesticks?" Kirsten asked. She looked around the bare little cabin. "We all need the heavy quilts and our warm clothes for winter. And Papa needs his hand tools, and I need Sari. Or at least I miss her. Don't you miss your things, too?"

Mama patted the last loaf of bread and set it on the tray. "People are more important than things, Kirsten."

Kirsten traced a heart shape in the flour on the table. "You always say that, Mama. But things help me remember people, too. When I wear my sweater from Mormor, I can picture her knitting it for me. If I could see the Christmas cloths you both wove for the rafters, I'd feel like she was here with us."

Mama had the dough tray halfway into the cupboard, but now she stopped and looked closely at Kirsten. Even in the dim cabin Mama's eyes were as blue as the cloudless sky. "You're a wise girl, Kirsten. Our things can have special meanings for us. They help us remember. I feel just as you do."

"You do?" Kirsten asked.

Mama nodded. "I often think of the day we finished packing the painted trunk to bring to America. Do you remember that day?"

"I remember it was spring and there were buds on the maple tree. Mormor and your friend Mrs. Hanson came early in the morning and stayed all day to help us," Kirsten said.

"We were used to working together," Mama said softly. "How carefully Mormor folded our sweaters. And Mrs. Hanson brought dried lavender to put in with our linens so they would smell sweet when we unpacked them here." Mama gazed at the window as though she could see Kirsten's grandmother and Mrs. Hanson right now.

"I remember how you all laughed when Peter begged to put his sled into the trunk," Kirsten said.

"And how we all cried when we said good-bye," Mama whispered. "We knew we would never see each other again."

Kirsten was surprised to see tears in Mama's

blue eyes. She didn't know that Mama could get homesick, too.

"Mama, are you all right?" Kirsten asked.

Abruptly, Mama turned and shoved the bread tray into the cupboard. "Of course I'm all right." She poured coffee into the coffee pail and held it out to Kirsten. "Now take this hot coffee out to the barn for Papa. He forgets to rest and warm himself unless we remind him. Let's get on with our work, Kirsten."

Papa stood in the back of the wagon to fork hay into the barn. His cheeks were red from work and from cold. He climbed down and took the coffee pail from Kirsten. "Just what I need," he said as he sipped the steaming coffee. Bits of hay stuck to his work jacket and his beard.

Kirsten leaned against the wagon wheel. "Papa, could you go to town tomorrow and get the trunks? Mama and I need some things from the painted trunk especially."

Papa glanced at Kirsten over the rim of the pail as he sipped. "When all our work is done here I'll go for the trunks," he said. "First things first."

Kirsten looked around at the wide fields. The farm was large, and she could see that there was still much to be done. "When will all the work be finished?" she asked.

"It *must* be done before the heavy snows come or we won't get through the winter. Now don't pester me, Kirsten," he said gruffly. But when he handed her back the empty coffee pail he patted her shoulder. "I'll get the trunks as soon as I have time."

But Papa didn't have time. The hogs had to be butchered and the meat smoked. Papa and Uncle Olav spent a whole week repairing fences. They put new runners on the sleigh and new shoes on the horse. In the evenings they mended harness leather and stuffed extra clay between the logs in the cabin walls to make the cabin warmer. They put up a fence to keep snowdrifts off the path to the barn. When the heavy snows came it would be too late to do these important things.

Kirsten knew that when the heavy snows came it would be too late to get the trunks, too. The drifts would block the road into Maryville, and the snow wouldn't melt until spring. She couldn't wait until spring to have Sari back! The more Kirsten thought about the trunks, the more reasons she found for wanting them. Surely Lars wanted his skates, and Peter wanted his clay whistle. And she thought that unpacking the painted trunk would be like a visit home to Sweden for Mama. Every night when she said her prayers she prayed that Papa would get the trunks soon.

A CROWN
FOR A QUEEN

Kirsten sat with Lisbeth and Anna in
a cozy corner of the barn. These days it
was much too cold to play in their fort
under the cherry tree, so they brought their dolls
inside and scooped out rooms for them in the sweet-
smelling hay. The barn cats prowled around,
switching their tails. But they were too wild to be
petted or put into doll dresses.

Kirsten was trying to make a dress for Little
Sari. She wrapped Little Sari in one of Papa's white
handkerchiefs and tied a piece of red yarn around
it for a sash. Then she pretended to walk Little Sari
across the hay to Anna. "Do you think Little Sari
looks like Saint Lucia?" she asked Anna.

11

Anna looked up in surprise. "Who?"

"Saint Lucia. Don't you know Saint Lucia?" Kirsten asked, puzzled.

Anna shook her head. "Is she someone you knew in Sweden?"

Now Kirsten was really startled. "No, Anna. We celebrated Saint Lucia's Day in Sweden. It was the very best part of Christmas."

"I don't remember Sweden," Lisbeth said. "I was just a baby when Mama left. We just celebrate Christmas Day."

Kirsten's spirits fell. She'd hoped this first Christmas in America would be just like Christmas in Sweden. How could it, if they didn't have Saint Lucia's Day? She thought Mama would be disappointed, too. It was her favorite celebration.

"Tell us about Saint Lucia's Day," Anna said. She sat her doll on her lap as though the doll listened, too.

"In Sweden, Saint Lucia's Day begins the Christmas season," Kirsten explained. "It's the darkest day of the whole year. It's so dark that there's only daylight for a few hours. But no one minds the dark, because Saint Lucia's Day is such fun."

12

"Tell us about Saint Lucia's Day,"
Anna said.

13

Lisbeth was braiding a straw belt for her doll. "What do you do?"

"In each family, one girl gets to be the Lucia queen. She dresses up in a long white dress and a red sash, and she wears a crown of green leaves and lighted candles. She gets up very, very early in the morning, while it's still pitch black and everyone is asleep. She lights the candles in her crown, and she goes from room to room in the dark house, carrying a tray. First she goes to her parents' room. Even though they've helped her get ready, they can hardly believe their eyes when they see her, she looks so beautiful in her costume. Then she wakes all the rest of the family and invites them to share Lucia buns and coffee. That breakfast is the first party of the holiday season," Kirsten explained.

Anna's gray eyes grew wider and she hugged herself. "Oh, a white dress and a crown! It sounds beautiful. I wish *we* had Saint Lucia's Day."

That gave Kirsten an idea. She motioned for her cousins to draw closer together. "Why don't we make a Saint Lucia's celebration? Just the three of us!

14

We won't tell our parents or the boys. We'll get everything ready and surprise them. Wouldn't that be fun?"

Anna's round face glowed with excitement. "We'll keep it a secret! Oh, I love secrets!"

But Lisbeth cocked her head and frowned. "It would be exciting, all right. But how could we get all the special things we'd need?"

"That won't be hard," Kirsten insisted. "Mama always has coffee, and we can slice a loaf of our Christmas bread and pretend it's Lucia buns. That takes care of the tray."

"How about the crown?" Lisbeth asked.

"I think we could make one from a wild grapevine and wintergreen leaves. It shouldn't be too hard to do." As Kirsten planned, she grew more and more excited.

Now Anna was too eager to sit still. She hopped to her feet and waved her arms, and the cats scattered and hissed. "You can be Saint Lucia, Kirsten, because you know how," Anna cried.

"But where will we get a white dress and red sash?" asked Lisbeth.

"I have a white dress!" Kirsten answered.

15

"Well, it's really a white nightdress, but it's just what we need. I wore it last year for Saint Lucia's Day. It's in our trunk."

Now the three girls looked at each other in silence. Then they each let out a sigh. "But your trunks aren't *here*," Lisbeth said.

"When is Saint Lucia's Day?" Anna asked.

"It's December thirteenth," Kirsten said. Quickly she counted on her fingers. "That's five whole days from now."

Lisbeth shrugged sadly. "Then it's no use planning. If your father doesn't get that trunk, there's no white dress and sash."

Anna let herself tumble backward into the hay. When she got up, hay was stuck in her braids. "It was a grand idea. But we don't have candles for the crown, either. Mama would surely miss them if we took them without asking her."

But now Kirsten was determined to make a Saint Lucia celebration. She *had* to think of something. Of course! They could ask Miss Winston!

Kirsten got to her knees and grabbed Anna's ankle to get her attention. "We could ask Miss

16

Winston to get us some candles and to help us."
Miss Winston was the teacher at Powderkeg School.
She'd been living at Uncle Olav's house for several
weeks and would stay there all winter, until she
moved in with another family.

Anna grinned. "Oh, I know Miss Winston would
like a party. She's been telling us about the Christmas
parties they had back East. It makes her sad to think
she'll miss them. And she has extra candles in her
trunk!"

"That still leaves the dress," Lisbeth said slowly.
"I don't know . . ."

"Lisbeth, Papa practically promised me that he'd
get the trunks soon," Kirsten said. "We'll make all
the things we need, and we'll practice. When he gets
the trunks, we'll be ready!"

Lisbeth looked relieved. "We should start getting
everything ready now. We'll have to practice up in
our room so the boys won't know what we're doing."

"And we'll have to hide the crown under the
bed, won't we?" Anna cried. "Or under Miss
Winston's bed. They'd never look there!"

Suddenly Lisbeth held her finger to her lips.
"Shhhhh!"

Kirsten listened. She heard the cows mooing and Papa's deep voice as he brought them in to be milked. "It's Papa," she whispered.

"Go right now and ask him to get the trunks," Lisbeth said. "Tell him it's important!"

Kirsten took a deep breath. She knew how Papa hated to be pestered. But she had to ask him about the trunks one more time. She climbed out of the hay and went over to Papa, who sat on a small stool milking a brown cow. He leaned his forehead against the cow's side. Steam rose from the pail of warm milk.

"Papa, I've been thinking about our trunks again. Can't you *please* get them soon?" Kirsten said.

Papa's breath was a white cloud at his lips. He raised his eyebrows. "Just why are the trunks so important, Kirsten?"

Kirsten stubbed her boot against the empty bucket. "I remembered our candlesticks are in the painted trunk. Mama will want the candlesticks for Christmas."

"We all want things we can't have. I've heard enough about that trunk," Papa said. He squirted

a stream of milk into the mouth of the gray cat by
Kirsten's feet.

"*Please*, Papa."

Now Papa scowled. "Don't ask me again or
I'll be angry!"

Kirsten walked slowly to the stall where Blackie,
Uncle Olav's horse, munched hay. She patted his
coat, which was thickened against the cold. "What
can I do now?" she murmured to Blackie. "Everything depends on that trunk." Blackie snuffled and
pushed his soft nose against her hand as though he
sensed she needed comfort.

On the way home from school the next day,
Kirsten cut a length of grapevine and Lisbeth picked
wintergreen. They took them to Anna and Lisbeth's
sleeping loft to work on the Saint Lucia crown.

Miss Winston was there. She sat on her bed
to grade arithmetic tests. "Of course you may use
some of my candles," she said when they asked her
for them. She took three new candles from the trunk

at the foot of her bed and cut them in two to make them the right length. "I'll hide the crown in my trunk, if you like," Miss Winston added. "I like surprises, too."

So that part was easy. But making the crown was harder. The first crown Lisbeth braided was too small. "It looks like a bird's nest," Anna said when she saw it perched on top of Kirsten's head.

The second crown Lisbeth made was much too large. It slipped right down over Kirsten's head and lay around her neck. "And that one looks like Blackie's harness," Anna told her.

"Measure Kirsten's head first," Miss Winston suggested. She gave Lisbeth a piece of string.

Lisbeth tied the string around Kirsten's head. Then she braided the grapevine exactly the size of the circle of string. This time the crown fit perfectly. Lisbeth stuck sprigs of wintergreen into the braided vine and Miss Winston set the candles in securely.

Then they decided how the tray would be laid out. "We'll have coffee and Christmas bread, and a candle in the center. All the lights will be out except for the candles," Kirsten said. "Saint Lucia comes into a dark room with her crown glowing!"

Anna put the crown on her own head and pretended to carry a tray. She walked slowly around the room. "What does Saint Lucia say now?" she asked.

"Say, 'Saint Lucia invites you to breakfast,'" Kirsten told her.

Anna cried, "Oh, this is fun!"

Lisbeth came to sit on the bed beside Kirsten. She took Kirsten's hand. "This *is* a good plan, really it is. If your trunk doesn't come in time for Saint Lucia's Day, we can have the celebration next year. Don't worry, Kirsten," Lisbeth said.

But Kirsten couldn't help but worry. She had butterflies in her stomach. She'd gotten everyone's hopes up, especially her own. And she was afraid to ask Papa about the trunk again. She would just have to wait and see what happened. There was nothing else she could do now.

TO TOWN
AT LAST

On Tuesday, Kirsten woke to the
sound of voices. Except for the fire in
the stove, the cabin was so dark and
cold that she could see her breath. From her bed, she
saw that thick ice covered the little window. Peter
and Lars still slept, their heads almost hidden under
their covers. But Mama and Papa were up. They sat
at the pine table, talking softly. Kirsten stayed under
her quilt and listened.

"We finished putting up the snow fences
yesterday," Papa said. "I think we were just in time.
It looks like we'll have another heavy snow soon.
But I could drive into town today. Olav won't need
the horse. What do you think?"

"If it's safe to go, you should try. One more hard snow and the roads will be blocked until spring," Mama said.

"Will you pack me a lunch, then? I'll leave as soon as the milking is done and be back with the trunks before suppertime," Papa said.

The trunks! Now Kirsten was wide awake, her heart pounding. Tomorrow was Saint Lucia's Day! They would get the trunks just in time!

She was out of her bed with a leap. She ran across the rough boards of the cabin floor and threw her arms around Mama's neck. "Oh, Mama, please may I go along in the wagon to get our trunks? It doesn't matter if I miss one day of school!"

Papa was already pulling on his heavy boots. "There's too much snow for the wagon. I'm going to hitch Blackie to the sleigh, and there's not much room in that small sleigh, Kirsten."

"But *I* don't take up much room!" Kirsten cried.

"It's a long drive. You'll get cold. Go to school with your brothers," Papa said.

"But I want to go with you more than anything in the world, Papa!"

"Do you want to come with me that much?"

Papa asked. "What will you do?"

"I can help you, I'm sure of it. I can keep you company so you won't get lonely," Kirsten said. "Please say yes!"

She thought Papa might scowl because he didn't like to be urged to change his mind. But instead he laughed. "You have a strong will, Kirsten! Just like your mama! You may come with me. Eat your breakfast and dress in your warmest clothes, then bring in a bucket of snow so Mama will have water today. I'll hitch up the sleigh and we'll be on our way. Hurry, now."

Kirsten hurried. She put on two pairs of wool stockings, all of her quilted petticoats, her heaviest sweater, and a shawl. As she ate her pancakes, she watched Mama pack a lunch in the hamper and heat stones in the oven. The warm stones would keep Kirsten's and Papa's feet cozy in the sleigh.

The first rays of light came through the clouds as Papa brought the sleigh from the barn. Kirsten climbed into the sleigh beside Papa, and Mama handed her the food hamper. "Here's your lunch. And I put in a loaf of Christmas bread for you to

24

give Mr. Berkhoff at the store. We might not see him again until spring. Tell him we wish him a happy Christmas."

Mama stood by the gate and waved as the sleigh pulled away down the road. "Take care!" she called after them.

Blackie whinnied and stamped. The harness bells around his neck jingled merrily. Kirsten laughed with pleasure when she heard the bells. She remembered the wonderful holidays in Sweden, the sleigh rides they'd taken to church and to the homes of their friends.

Snow was falling as Kirsten and Papa left the farm. The snowflakes settled on Blackie's back like moths and caught in Kirsten's eyelashes. Papa turned the horse east toward the small town of Maryville. Now the wind was at their backs. Under a fur blanket, Kirsten was snug by Papa's side.

Papa's wide-brimmed hat was pulled low. He wore his sheepskin mittens with high tops that came up over his jacket cuffs, and a red scarf Mama had knitted for him. As they slid along, he began to sing a Christmas carol. His deep voice seemed to fill up his whole chest and to push ahead of them through

the softly falling snow.

Kirsten sang, too. She was happy. In no time they'd pick up their trunks and be back at the farm. Then, tomorrow morning before dawn, she and Lisbeth and Anna would surprise everyone with the Saint Lucia celebration. Their plans were turning out perfectly after all.

By the time they reached Maryville it was snowing harder. The soft snow made caps on the tops of the fenceposts and piled up on the shingled rooftops. Kirsten and Papa drove past houses, the church, and the sawmill, then stopped in front of Berkhoff's General Store. While Papa unhitched Blackie from the sleigh, Kirsten watched the men and women in the street. She was glad to smell woodsmoke in the air and to hear people greeting one another. Maryville was only a little town, but it had a happy bustle.

Inside the store, the delicious scents of spices, new cloth, oiled leather, and sausages reached Kirsten's nose all at once. Mr. Berkhoff stood behind the scales, weighing sugar. When he saw Kirsten and Papa, he wiped his hands on his white apron and came around the counter to shake Papa's hand. He gave Kirsten a piece of hard sugar candy from one of the glass jars. "It's not Christmas yet, but have a little treat," he said.

Kirsten handed him the loaf of Christmas bread Mama had sent. "Mama sends you a merry Christmas greeting," she said. "And thank you for the candy."

Mr. Berkhoff raised his white eyebrows.

"Kirsten Larson, the last time you were in my store you spoke to me in Swedish!"

Kirsten felt herself blush. "I'm learning English."

"So you are! And you speak it very well, too," Mr. Berkhoff said. "Thank your mother for the bread."

"We're here to pick up our trunks," Papa said.

"Come with me," Mr. Berkhoff said. He took them to a big storage room at the back of the store. Wooden boxes and barrels were piled clear up to the ceiling. Mr. Berkhoff pushed aside some crates to let Kirsten and Papa through. There, by the back door, they saw the two big trunks with "Anders Larson" painted on their sides.

Papa slapped the trunks with his open hand the way he slapped the cows. "Well, Kirsten, here are our things at last!"

Kirsten leaned against the painted trunk. She traced the flower paintings with her fingertip. Sari was in this trunk—right there under the lid. The white nightdress and red sash she needed for Saint Lucia's Day would be near all of Mama's lovely weavings. And at the bottom of the trunk there were heavy woolen sweaters, caps, mittens, and the shiny brass candlesticks. Oh, everything was in this trunk! It seemed like an old dear friend Kirsten had met again after a long time. She pressed her cheek against the rounded top.

"Papa, let's open the trunk now!" she said. "I want to hold Sari on the sleigh ride home."

Papa and Mr. Berkhoff pushed the trunks out the back door onto the loading platform. "We'll open the trunks when we get them home," Papa said. "We've got to go right now. It's snowing harder, and we have a long drive back home."

Mr. Berkhoff squinted up into the snow. "Maybe you folks should stay here until the snow stops, Mr. Larson."

"Thank you," Papa said, "but I think we'll leave now before this snow gets heavier."

"Don't get lost," Mr. Berkhoff warned. "This looks like it will be a storm." He lifted Kirsten into the sleigh beside Papa.

"Merry Christmas!" Kirsten called back to Mr. Berkhoff as Papa drove the sleigh away from the store.

Mr. Berkhoff's answering call was muffled by the thud of Blackie's steps in the snow. "Merry Christmas to you, too!"

BRAVING THE
BLIZZARD

 As they left Maryville in the loaded sleigh, the snow seemed to fall harder every minute. It stung Kirsten's cheeks until she pulled her shawl up over her nose. Papa urged Blackie faster, but now the horse had the extra weight of the trunks to pull and the sleigh didn't skim along as it had done before. "Look at that sky!" Papa said. "The weather changed while we waited in the store."

When the road turned west toward the farm, Kirsten saw that the sleigh tracks they'd made earlier were filling with snow. The strong wind drove the snow directly into their faces. There was no way to hide from it.

"Pull the blanket over your head," Papa told Kirsten.

She curled up next to Papa's side and buried her face under his arm. She could hear the thump of Papa's heart and the muffled jingle of the sleigh bells as Blackie trotted along.

The next time Kirsten peeked over the edge of the blanket all she could see was white. Snow swirled up from the fields like spray blown from the tops of waves. Drifts shifted and moved as Blackie stepped along. Papa's beard was filled with snow, his mustache was white with it. His eyes were blue slits under his snow-caked eyebrows.

"Where's the road, Papa?" Kirsten asked.

"I can't see it. We're following the fenceposts. Blackie can find his way, though. He's a smart horse," Papa said.

"Do you think we should go back to Maryville?"

"We've already come a long way. I think there's a better chance the horse knows his way to the farm. If we just keep heading west we'll be all right." But Papa frowned into the fiercely blowing snow.

Kirsten was worried, too. She'd heard stories about settlers who lost their way in blizzards and walked in circles until they fell down. She'd heard about a boy who froze to death when he got lost between his barn and his house. A snowstorm on the plains was as dangerous as a storm on the ocean.

Blackie's harness bells sounded faint and lost. His ears were down, his head low. Papa urged him to keep going, but the horse often stumbled in the moving drifts. Kirsten's feet were so cold she could barely move her toes. Under her feet, she felt the stones Mama had heated that morning. The warmth had long since gone out of them.

"Toss the stones out of the sleigh," Papa told her. "We should make this load lighter. The trunks are heavier than I remembered."

"But we won't leave our trunks in the snow, will we?" Kirsten asked.

Papa patted her knee. "No, we won't leave our trunks. This snow will let up soon, you'll see." He slapped the reins against Blackie's back, which was thickly covered with snow.

Then there were no more fenceposts to follow.

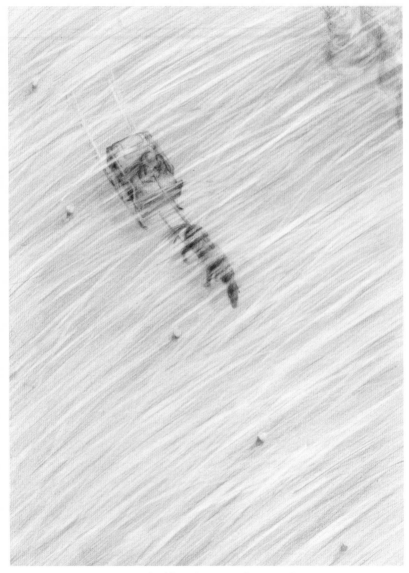

Kirsten had heard stories about settlers
who lost their way in blizzards.

They drove along beside a dim shadow that
Kirsten knew was the edge of the forest. But
Blackie walked more and more slowly.
Often Papa had to flick the whip across
his back to keep him moving.

"He wants to turn his back to the wind," Papa
said. "But we have to go straight into the wind if
we're going to get back to the farm."

"Keep going, Blackie!" Kirsten shouted. Her
words seemed to disappear into the snow and wind.

All at once Blackie stopped. He wouldn't move.
"Yo!" Papa yelled. "Get up there!"

It was no use. The horse wouldn't take a single
step.

"What's wrong with him?" Kirsten asked.

"He loses his footing in the snow, and that
frightens him," Papa said. "I'll have to lead him to
keep him moving."

Papa handed Kirsten the reins, wrapped the
blanket tightly around her waist, and climbed down
from the sleigh. He stepped through snowdrifts to
Blackie's head and took hold of his bridle. "Come
on, Blackie! Come along, now!" Papa made his
voice both gruff and soothing. The horse took one

step, stopped, then took another step. The bells jingled again.

Kirsten realized she'd been holding her breath. She let it out with a sigh. Blackie trusted Papa. Now they'd keep going toward home.

They went slowly, step by difficult step. Papa climbed through knee-high drifts. Even though he was only a few feet in front of her, Kirsten could hardly see him. He was completely covered with snow. Papa pulled Blackie's bridle, and Kirsten slapped Blackie's flanks with the reins.

The snow and cold made Kirsten light-headed. Sometimes it seemed the sleigh wasn't moving at all. Only the snow seemed to move, like water running in a stream.

Then Papa stumbled. He went down on his knees and cried out. Kirsten had never heard Papa cry out in pain before, and the sound was colder than the wind.

"Papa!" she shouted. "Papa, are you all right?"

She jumped out of the sleigh. The snow came up to her hips, but Kirsten pushed through it to Papa's side.

Papa tried to stand, but again he went down in the snow.

"What's the matter, Papa?"

"My knee. I twisted my knee. I can't put my weight on it," he said. His face was very pale, his lips white. There was ice in his mustache.

"What can I do?" Kirsten begged him.

"Nothing, Kirsten. It's up to Blackie now," Papa answered. "We can't stop here. We have to reach shelter." He dragged himself back to the sleigh, breathing hard. Kirsten wondered how he would ever get back onto the high front seat.

At last Papa managed to crawl up. Then he reached down to help Kirsten up beside him. But when he snapped the whip over Blackie's back, the horse wouldn't budge.

"It's no good," Papa said. "With no one to lead him, he'll stay right here."

Kirsten grabbed Papa's hand. "But *I* can lead Blackie!" she said. "You stay in the sleigh, and I'll walk beside him."

"Do you think you can walk through this deep snow?"

"I'll try, Papa!"

Papa brushed the snow off Kirsten's shoulders and tied her shawl more tightly over her nose and mouth. Then he pulled off his sheepskin mittens and put them on her hands. Inside Papa's mittens the fleece was warm and dry. Kirsten's cold hands felt like rabbits creeping into a snug home.

"You're a good girl, Kirsten," Papa said. "You have heart."

Papa had told Mama she had heart when she agreed to come here to America. He told Mama she had heart when she was sick on the ship but didn't lose hope. Kirsten wanted to be as brave as Mama. She pulled herself along Blackie's side. She shook the harness and made the bells sound. "Yo!" she cried in the biggest voice she could manage. "Yo, Blackie! Come along!" To her surprise, the horse's head came up and he followed her.

But the going was hard. Kirsten's feet slipped. The drifts were up to her knees, and now her feet were so numb she couldn't even wiggle her toes. Like the horse, she bent her head into the wind and concentrated on just one step, then the next, then the next.

Snow caked on her lips. *Keep going*, she told herself. *Have heart, Kirsten.* But she didn't know where she was going. The whole world was a white blowing snowdrift. And it would soon be dark. Then how would they ever, ever find the way home?

Kirsten tried to imagine their home, the little snug cabin somewhere in this storm. It would be warm there. She imagined Mama making soup for supper. She imagined Lisbeth and Anna waiting to make the Saint Lucia's Day surprise.

Keep going, Kirsten told herself. She tried to sing a Christmas carol to keep her spirits up. But her lips were so cold she could barely move them. Instead, she began to count the way Miss Winston drilled numbers in school. *One, two, three, four*—that was four steps closer to home. *Five, six, seven, eight*—eight steps closer to home. Kirsten was glad she'd learned her numbers. Maybe the numbers would keep her moving. *Nine, ten, eleven*—she bumped into something. She fell against Blackie's side and looked around. They weren't in the fields near the forest anymore. They were near some rocks.

"We've come the wrong way," Papa called. "The horse has taken us into a valley by the stream. He's lost."

Kirsten shielded her eyes from the snow to look. She knew where they were! Blackie hadn't come the wrong way at all! These were the cliffs she'd gone to with Singing Bird, her Indian friend. There was the forked birch tree, bent over by the wind. She knew that tree! She'd passed it on her way to the cave where she and Singing Bird had sometimes played.

Kirsten struggled back to Papa. She reached

40

up and grabbed his hand. "I know where we are, Papa!"

"How can you know where we are, Kirsten? The horse has lost his way."

"I've been here!" Kirsten cried.

"You've been here? Where are we?" Papa asked.

"We're beside a cliff. There's a tiny cave nearby." Kirsten pointed.

Papa looked up at the cliff. "How far to the cave?"

"It's only a little way. And there's dry wood inside. We can stay there until the storm is over," Kirsten said.

Papa tried to stand, but his leg gave out and he sat down again. "Can you take care of Blackie?" he asked.

"Yes, I'm sure I can."

"Then unharness him from the sleigh and lead him to that clump of birch trees. He'll rest there and be glad of it." Groaning, Papa crawled down from the sleigh. He sat on the snow and pushed himself backwards, inching up the slope toward the opening of the cave.

As Papa climbed, Kirsten took Blackie's harness off. It was hard to do in Papa's big mittens, so she pulled one off and held it in her teeth while she worked at the buckle. Blackie followed her a few yards to the shelter of the clump of trees. As she tied his reins to the birch tree, he whinnied.

Kirsten brushed the snow from his forelock and his face. "Good old Blackie! You have heart, do you know that? You're a very brave horse!" Then she followed Papa up the path to the cave.

Inside, the cave was dry and not very deep. Near the back was a pile of dry sticks and grass, and the black traces of campfires the Indians had made. Singing Bird had said that they sometimes stayed here when they were hunting.

Papa twisted a handful of dry grass, then laid dry sticks over it. He chipped at a piece of stone with his flint until he got sparks. A tiny flame began in the dry grass. Papa blew gently and the sticks caught fire. Kirsten brought a larger branch and laid it by the little fire.

"First we must warm up your feet, Kirsten. Take

"When did you come to this cave?"
Papa asked.

off your boots," Papa said. He leaned against the dry wall of the cave.

Kirsten spread the blanket next to Papa, sat down, and loosened her bootlaces. When she got her boots off, Papa began to rub her feet gently with his warm hands. Soon her toes started to tingle. She knew it was a good sign that they hurt—they weren't frozen.

Papa took off his own boots now and put a thick log on the fire. "When did you come to this cave?" he asked her.

Because Kirsten didn't want to tell him about Singing Bird and the Indians, she said, "I was exploring along the stream, and I found it."

"Did you have permission to be so far from the farm?" Papa asked sternly.

Kirsten shook her head. "No, Papa. I wandered farther than I thought."

The ice was melting from Papa's beard, and she saw that he smiled at her. "I'm glad that you're a little explorer, Kirsten. I'm glad you found this cave. Do you think you can find your way back to the farm from here?"

"I think so, Papa."

"Then lie back and rest," Papa said. "There's nothing we can do until it stops snowing, and you must be very, very tired."

Now that they were resting, Kirsten realized she was hungry. She was too exhausted to climb down the path and get what was left of their lunch from the sleigh. But in her pocket she found the piece of sugar candy Mr. Berkhoff had given her at the general store. The candy was shaped like a Christmas bell. She put it in her mouth and lay down beside Papa. The last thing she knew before she fell into a deep sleep was the taste of cinnamon and sugar on her tongue.

SILENT NIGHT, LUCIA LIGHT

When Kirsten woke, Papa was brushing dirt on the fire to put it out. Outside, it was very dark. The night sky was clear, but there was no moon. "The storm's gone past," Papa said. "Now we can make our way home if you can lead Blackie. I still can't stand on my leg."

Kirsten rubbed her eyes and sat up. "I can lead him," she said. She rolled up the blanket, and Papa helped her into her boots, which he'd warmed by the fire. While Papa crawled slowly down the path, she untied Blackie and hitched him to the sleigh.

The fresh snow gleamed in the starlight. *It must be very late if the moon has gone down*, Kirsten thought. She imagined Mama peering out of the

46

cabin window, looking for them. Mama would be worried.

As Kirsten led Blackie beside the stream, she watched for familiar landmarks. From time to time she looked back at Papa in the sleigh and at the painted trunk under its roof of snow. The sleigh bells jingled crisply in the still night.

At last Kirsten recognized a big oak tree and the curve in the stream where she'd often met Singing Bird. But the woods looked different in the deep snow. Was this the place where they should turn to find the farm? She hesitated. Blackie nudged her with his nose. Yes, this must be the way.

Before Kirsten saw the cabin and Uncle Olav's house, she smelled woodsmoke. Then they came around a turn and she saw that candles lit up all the windows of Uncle Olav's house. Everyone was waiting there. They had stayed up all night to look for her and Papa.

Kirsten led Blackie right up to Uncle Olav's door. As they approached, Papa shouted, "We're here! We're safe!"

Faces appeared at all the windows. The door

swung wide, and Mama ran out. "Here you are at
last. We were so worried," she said as she hugged
Kirsten. "But you're hurt!" she added when she saw
Papa. She climbed into the sleigh to hug him, too.

Everyone crowded around the sleigh, asking
questions. Uncle Olav helped Papa down from the
sleigh, and Aunt Inger said, "I'll heat some soup to
warm your chilly bones." Lisbeth, Anna, and Miss
Winston all hugged Kirsten, and even Lars squeezed
her shoulder before he went to untie the trunks.
Peter was jumping up and down in front of the
stove. "We stayed up all night to watch for you!
Even Miss Winston stayed up all night," he said.

For a moment, Kirsten stood in the doorway
to the kitchen and just stared. It seemed to her that
she and Papa had been gone for days instead of
hours. And now the world seemed turned upside
down. It was the middle of the night, but in the
kitchen, where all the lamps were lit, it was as
bright as day. Aunt Inger bustled about heating
the potato soup, but everyone was
wearing nightclothes. Kirsten smiled
to see Uncle Olav with his nightshirt
tucked into his trousers and his

sleeping cap still on his head. She smiled to see Anna in her nightgown and Mama's sweater, which trailed down to the floor. Even Miss Winston's hair was unbraided, although she had gotten dressed.

At last Kirsten sat near the warm stove with a bowl of hot soup in front of her. Mama hugged her once more, so hard she was nearly lifted from her chair. "Oh, I knew you shouldn't have gone with Papa to fetch the trunks," Mama said.

But Papa said, "Be glad Kirsten came with me. She's a brave girl, and a strong one. If she hadn't been along to help me, I'd never have found the cave or my way home."

Mama put her arm around Papa's waist. "I can believe that Kirsten is as brave as her papa. Come sit down here and rest your leg. I'll bring you some soup." She smiled at Kirsten. "Don't let yours get cold."

Anna and Lisbeth came to sit by Kirsten as she ate. "We were so frightened for you," Anna said. "Our papa wanted to go out in the storm to search for you, but Mama said he'd never find you on foot. We didn't know what to do! Were you scared?"

Kirsten sipped the thick soup. "I was scared. Then I was too busy to be scared anymore. Anyway, we're here now and we've got the trunk!" Under the table she gave Anna's hand a squeeze.

Anna put her head close to Kirsten's. "You don't want to have our surprise *now,* do you?"

Kirsten grinned. "This is Saint Lucia's Day and it's the perfect time," she whispered. "Saint Lucia is supposed to wake everyone at four in the morning. It must be about four now."

Lisbeth pulled her chair closer. "But how will we surprise everyone when they're all awake anyway?" she asked.

Kirsten lowered her voice even more. "When Lars and Uncle Olav bring the trunk in, Mama is sure to want to open it. I'll sneak the white dress out. In the meantime, you can get the crown and the tray of bread. When we're all ready, Miss Winston can tell everyone to shut their eyes. How will that be?"

"It's a grand idea!" Anna said. "I'll whisper to Miss Winston what she's supposed to do."

Lars and Uncle Olav carried the painted trunk into the middle of the cabin. When Uncle Olav lifted

the lid, the sweet scent of dried lavender filled the air. Kirsten hurried to Mama's side.

Mama reached into the trunk and out came Sari. Mama gave the doll a little hug and handed her to Kirsten. "I know how much you missed your doll, Kirsten. Last night I missed you and Papa even more. Now we're all together again, even Sari."

Kirsten took Sari in both hands and looked at her closely in the flickering light. Sari was just a rag doll with a faded face and a sun-bleached dress, but she was Kirsten's very, very own. Kirsten

51

pressed Sari to her cheek.

"And here's Peter's clay whistle," Mama said.

Papa smiled and held his finger to his lips. Peter had fallen asleep beside him.

"This has been such a long night," Mama said gently to Papa. "You must be exhausted. Let's all get some sleep and finish unpacking the trunk later."

Anna leaned around the end of the trunk and tugged Kirsten's skirt. "*Do* something!" she whispered.

"At least find the sweaters from Mormor," Kirsten said to Mama. "And the pillow covers you wove for Aunt Inger. Unpack at least that much."

Mama didn't need to be urged. Piece by piece, she began to lift their precious things from the trunk. She handed them to Aunt Inger, who laid them on the table.

Kirsten watched for her chance. While Aunt Inger was exclaiming over the pillow covers, Kirsten slipped the white nightdress from the trunk and handed it to Anna. The red sash was right next to it, inside Peter's cap. Anna shoved them both under her sweater.

Out of the corner of her eye, Kirsten saw Lisbeth climbing down the ladder from the loft. She had their crown and the candles wrapped in a quilt.

The girls met at the far end of the kitchen by the door into the shed. "Here's the tray!" Lisbeth said. "And Miss Winston's ready. Quick, put on the dress, it's cold!"

Kirsten slipped off her dress and shawl and pulled the white nightdress over her head. Next came the red sash. Finally, Lisbeth fitted the crown on Kirsten's head and lit the candles.

"Oh, Kirsten!" Anna breathed. "You look like an angel!"

"We're almost ready now," Lisbeth said as she lit the candle on the tray.

Miss Winston came hurrying into the kitchen. "I told everyone to shut their eyes, then I turned down the lamps. Come now, they're waiting!"

Anna and Lisbeth scampered across the kitchen ahead of Kirsten. Kirsten lifted her head high, took a deep breath, and walked slowly, holding the tray of coffee and bread. The big room was dim except for the light of her crown. Kirsten paused in the doorway. She saw everyone waiting with their eyes

"Saint Lucia invites you to breakfast!"
Kirsten said.

54

closed, as Miss Winston had asked them to do.

"Saint Lucia invites you to breakfast!" Kirsten said.

For just a moment the room was still. The only sound was the crackle of the fire in the stove. Then the commotion began.

Peter rubbed his eyes. "Oh, it's Christmas time!" he cried. Everyone called out "Merry Christmas!" and "What a wonderful surprise!"

Kirsten looked around the room as she passed the Saint Lucia tray to her family. Mama's blue eyes were shining. Aunt Inger and Uncle Olav were smiling with pleasure. Peter and Lars grinned and munched their bread. Miss Winston squeezed Anna's hand.

"Is this what it was like last Christmas in Sweden?" Lisbeth asked Kirsten as she handed Papa a mug of coffee.

Kirsten thought a moment about how much she'd loved the home she'd left behind in Sweden. Then she smiled at the cousins she liked so well. How happy she'd been tonight when she and Papa had finally found their way back to this new home, which was brightly lit for them in the dark.

"It's almost the same, but this year I think it's even better," she told Lisbeth. "Yes, it *is* a better Christmas. I think it's the best one of all."

LOOKING BACK

CHRISTMAS
IN
1854

A Swedish family at Christmas time, 1855

On the American frontier, Christmas was a time for special celebration. Settlers like the Larsons had a lot to celebrate. They had found new homes. They had good food, good health, and good neighbors. They were building new lives in America, including new American Christmas traditions.

Just as people on the frontier taught one another good ways to farm, build houses, and care for animals, they also shared their ways of celebrating Christmas. Kirsten told her cousins about the Swedish tradition of Saint Lucia. In return, Anna and Lisbeth probably showed her how they celebrated Christmas on their Minnesota farm. Their

A family celebrating Saint Lucia's Day

first Christmas in America would be a cheerful mix of old and new, Swedish and American traditions.

For families living in frontier towns in 1854, there were Christmas fairs and dances, church suppers, door-to-door caroling, and moonlight sleigh rides. But families who lived on farms had to make their own Christmas cheer. Their celebrations were quiet because frontier farms were far away from towns and from one another. Their celebrations were simple because work always came first on the farm. Cows had to be milked, horses had to be fed, fences had to be mended, and firewood had to be chopped, even at Christmas time. Pioneer families like the Larsons couldn't celebrate Christmas for a whole month, as they had in Sweden, because there was too much work to do just to survive.

Sleigh riding was a social activity as well as a means of transportation.

Winter was hard in Minnesota, and the bitter cold, the wind, and the snow were always dangerous enemies. Still, pioneers found some extra time to make

Christmas special. Mothers and daughters started to prepare for Christmas by scrubbing every inch of the house, from top to bottom. They washed all the clothes and quilts and curtains and hung them out in the brisk, clean December wind. Cabins would smell

A pioneer kitchen was busy at Christmas time.

delicious as special Christmas foods were prepared. Mama would have taught Kirsten how to make breads, cookies, spiced meats, and cheeses from her favorite Swedish Christmas recipes. Aunt Inger might have shown Kirsten and Mama how to cook a frontier feast of wild turkey stuffed with dried berries. Miss Winston could have introduced them to pumpkin pie and Yankee cornbread. By 1854, Christmas decorations on the frontier came from many different countries. Some immigrant families decorated their cabins so that they looked like their

Crisp, spicy pepparkakor cookies were a Swedish holiday favorite.

Swedish immigrants hung hand-woven cloths in their cabins

homes in the old country. Mama would have draped bright woven cloths over the rafters and polished her brass candlesticks until they glowed, just as she had in Sweden. German immigrants introduced other pioneers to everyone's favorite Christmas decoration, the Christmas tree.

Children like Anna, Lisbeth, and Kirsten would have had a happy time decorating their tree with painted wooden hearts and little animals made from straw. They would have made ropes of dried berries, too.

Sometimes Swedish families in America decorated their barns for Christmas. They attached a large bunch of wheat to a long pole just outside the door. The wheat became a Christmas feast for the birds. Swedish tradition said that a large flock of birds at Christmas time meant a good harvest the next year. And a good harvest was always important to a frontier family.

Candles were too precious for pioneers to waste, but on Christmas Eve a family like the Larsons might

Christmas wheat for the birds

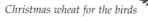

61

keep the Swedish tradition of lighting a candle in every window to show the way for *Jultomten* (YULE-tom-ten), the Swedish Christmas elf. He always visited on Christmas Eve. The gifts he brought to the American frontier would have been simple and useful. Perhaps there would be a pair of knitted socks, a hat, or a scarf. Part of the fun of *Jultomten's* visit came from

Jultomten was part of Christmas for Swedish children, just as Santa Claus is today.

the funny jokes, poems, and riddles written on the gifts he brought. Before children could open them, they had to try to guess what was inside. What do you think this present could be?

Red and white, soft as kittens,
These are for Kirsten,
A new pair of _____.

Frontier families tried very hard to get to church on Christmas Day. Services went on all day long. But snow, cold, and work kept many families on the farm all day. After their chores were done, a family like the Larsons might gather around their tree. They would sing hymns, read the story of the first Christmas from the Bible, and give thanks for the blessings of their first American Christmas.

A psalmodiken (sohl-MO-dih-ken), or Swedish one-stringed instrument

A Swedish hymnal, or church songbook

A SNEAK PEEK AT

HAPPY BIRTHDAY,
Kirsten!

Kirsten's mother is having a baby. When the baby starts to come early, it's up to Kirsten to go fetch help.

"irsten! Kirsten!" Mama was calling from their cabin. It was late morning, and Kirsten and Lisbeth were straining cheese curds in the shed next to the big house. Kirsten put down the strainer and went to see what Mama wanted.

In the dim cabin, Mama sat on the edge of the bed. Her hands were pressed against her big belly. There was sweat on her forehead, and she looked worried. "Where's your Aunt Inger?" she asked.

"She took a pot of soup to the Petersons because they've been so sick. She'll be back by noontime," Kirsten said.

"And where's Papa?"

"He and Uncle Olav are helping Mr. Peterson finish his planting." Kirsten looked at her mother curiously. Why was Mama asking all these questions? She knew as well as Kirsten what work had to be done today. She was the one who had told Kirsten and Lisbeth to strain cheese curds.

"They'll be back soon, won't they?" Mama asked.

"Yes, Mama. They'll be back in time for lunch. Is something wrong?"

Mama patted the bed beside her. "Sit with me for

a little while and keep me company. I think the baby is going to be born sooner than I expected. Maybe even today."

Kirsten's heart sped up and her mouth went dry. "Shouldn't I go fetch Aunt Inger to help you?"

"She'll be back soon. Just let me lie down and rest," Mama said.

Kirsten got the extra blanket and put it over Mama. Then she sat down beside her on the bed. Mama laced her fingers through Kirsten's. "Do you know what I thought about when I woke this morning?" Mama asked. Her eyes were a soft blue like the morning sky.

"What did you think about, Mama?"

Mama squeezed Kirsten's hand. "I remembered the day you were born, Kirsten. I remembered how my mother came to help me. Mrs. Hanson came, too. She helped all of us when we had babies. It was this time of year, late spring. New leaves were on the big maple tree outside the door. Then you were born, and Mrs. Hanson cleaned you and wrapped you in a blanket and put you in my arms. You were a red-faced little thing with white fuzz for hair. But I thought you were beautiful. I was so very, very happy because I wanted a daughter so much."

Kirsten put her head on her mother's shoulder. "Well, here I am," she said.

"Yes, here you are!" Mama smoothed the hair back from Kirsten's forehead. "And I was also thinking," Mama went on, stroking Kirsten's head, "that your birthday will be two weeks from this very day. June eighth. I'll never forget the day you were born."

So Mama did remember her birthday. How foolish Kirsten had been to think she would forget.

Suddenly, Mama squeezed Kirsten's hand extra hard. Kirsten sat up straight. "Are you all right, Mama?"

"This baby wants to be born whether we're ready or not. We'd better not wait for Inger to come home. You'd better go fetch her, and Papa, too."

"Can't I help you here?" Kirsten asked. Her heart was racing.

"Get Lisbeth to stay with me," Mama said. "You go for Aunt Inger and Papa. Will you do that for me?" Mama wiped the sweat from her face with a corner of the blanket.

"I'll take Blackie. I'll ride as fast as an Indian, Mama! I'll be right back with Aunt Inger and Papa! I promise!"

As Kirsten ran across the yard, she called, "Lisbeth, Mama's baby is coming and she needs you! Go quickly!" Then Kirsten dashed to the barn, grabbed Blackie's bridle, and chased him in from the pasture. "We have to hurry, Blackie!" she said as she pressed the bit between the horse's teeth. She climbed up the fence and onto his back.

Blackie liked to run. When Kirsten turned him into the lane and kicked him, he took off like a prairie fire. Kirsten leaned forward, and Blackie's mane whipped her face. She held on to his mane and the reins, and guided him with her knees. It wasn't far to the Petersons' cabin, maybe only two or three miles.

"Come on!" Kirsten urged the horse. Blackbirds swooped up from the fields as they passed. Blackie's hooves on the dirt lane pounded like a second heartbeat. "Let Mama be all right!" Kirsten prayed. "Please, let her be all right!"

Kirsten began calling, "Aunt Inger! Aunt Inger!" as she rode up to the Petersons' cabin.

"Oh, Aunt Inger," Kirsten said,
"please go as fast as you can!"

Aunt Inger was at the doorway in a moment. "Is it your mama's time?" she asked.

"She says to come quickly," Kirsten gasped. "Oh, Aunt Inger, please go as fast as you can!"

MORE TO DISCOVER! While books are the heart of

The American Girls Collection,® they are only the beginning. The stories

in the Collection come to life when you act them out with the beautiful American Girls dolls and their exquisite clothes and accessories. To request a free catalogue full of things girls love, send in this postcard, call **1-800-845-0005,** or visit our Web site at **americangirl.com**.

Please send me an American Girl®catalogue.

My name is _____

My address is _____

City _____ State _____ Zip _____

My birth date is _____/_____/_____ E-mail address _____
              month   day   year   *Fill in to receive updates and web-exclusive offers.*

Parent's signature _____

And send a catalogue to my friend.

My friend's name is _____

Address _____

City _____ State _____ Zip _____

If the postcard has already been removed from this book and you would like to receive an American Girl® catalogue, please send your name and address to:

American Girl
P.O. Box 620497
Middleton, WI 53562-0497

You may also call our toll-free number, **1-800-845-0005,** or visit our Web site at **americangirl.com**.

Place
Stamp
Here

PO BOX 620497
MIDDLETON WI 53562-0497